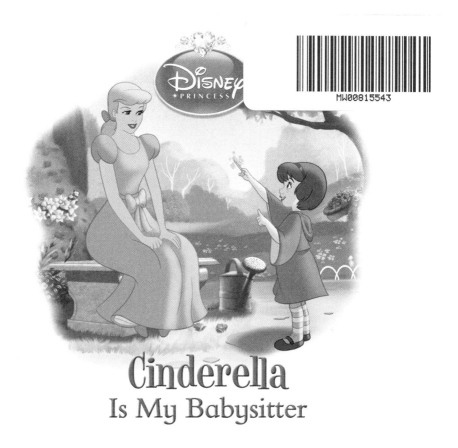

Cinderella
Is My Babysitter

By Andrea Posner-Sanchez
Illustrated by Fabio Laguna and Charles E. Pickens

 A GOLDEN BOOK • NEW YORK

randomhousekids.com
ISBN 978-0-7364-3324-2 (trade) — ISBN 978-0-7364-3325-9 (ebook)
Printed in the United States of America
10 9 8 7 6 5 4 3 2 1

One sunny day, Cinderella was out in the palace garden watering the flowers. Soon she noticed a cloud of twinkling lights falling gently to the ground. The princess smiled. She knew she was about to have a very special visitor.

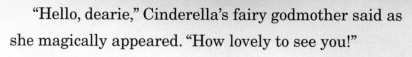

"Hello, dearie," Cinderella's fairy godmother said as she magically appeared. "How lovely to see you!"

"What brings you here today?" Cinderella asked.

"I was hoping you could look after my niece for just a spell," said the Fairy Godmother. "I'm planning a little surprise for her."

"It would be my pleasure," Cinderella replied.

The Fairy Godmother took out her magic wand and gave it a wave. In seconds, a young fairy girl appeared.

"Eliza, this is Cinderella," the Fairy Godmother said. "You two have fun together!" Then, with another wave of her wand, the Fairy Godmother was gone.

"Well, Eliza, what would you like to do?" Cinderella asked.

"Can I help you with your gardening?" asked Eliza.

"Of course," replied the princess. "I'll get us another watering can."

"That won't be necessary," said Eliza, raising her magic wand.

The little fairy pointed her wand at the watering can and shouted, "Bibbidi bobbidi spray!" In an instant, the watering can rose off the ground and began to water the flowers.

"That's amazing!" said Cinderella. The princess laughed as she and Eliza walked around the garden following the enchanted watering can.

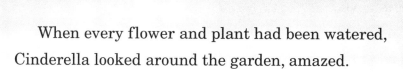

When every flower and plant had been watered, Cinderella looked around the garden, amazed.

"Either I'm shrinking or these flowers are growing extra fast!" she said.

Eliza giggled. "It's magic water," she admitted.

"Look what else I can do," Eliza said. The little fairy pointed her wand at the animal-shaped topiaries. "Bibbidi bobbidi move!"

Cinderella couldn't believe her eyes! A leafy elephant was swinging its trunk. And a leafy horse was galloping around and around the fountain.

Gus and Jaq scurried over.

"Is the circus in town, Jaq?" Gus asked, staring in awe
at the leafy animals.

Cinderella noticed her two little friends. "Gus and Jaq,
I'd like you to meet Eliza. She's the reason the garden is
extra-special today."

Eliza took out her wand to show the mice her magic skills. "Bibbidi bobbidi petals!" A burst of colorful flower petals floated down on Gus and Jaq like confetti. That was when the topiary elephant noticed the mice and got scared. It stood on its hind legs, made a loud trumpeting sound, and ran off!

The elephant trampled over flowers, knocked down trees, and crashed through fences.

"Oh, no!" cried Cinderella. "If it keeps going, it will run into the royal rose garden!"

Eliza felt awful. She took out her wand and shouted,
"Bibiddi bobbidi stop!" Nothing happened. She tried again.
"Bibbidi bobbidi come back!" But that didn't work, either.

Cinderella knew she needed to do something—and fast! The brave princess climbed onto the topiary horse and told Eliza not to do any more magic until she returned.

Cinderella held on to the horse's leafy mane and raced off. She caught up to the elephant just as it approached the fence surrounding the royal rose garden. Cinderella leapt off the horse and whistled. The elephant stopped in its tracks. She slowly walked up to it, speaking in a soothing voice.

"There's nothing to be scared of," she said. "Nothing at all."

Eliza was relieved to see the princess safely leading
the elephant and the horse back where they belonged.

"I'm so sorry, Cinderella," she called. "I'm the worst
fairy ever!"

"That's not true," Cinderella told her. "You simply need
more practice, that's all."

Just then, Eliza's aunt appeared.

"It is time for your surprise," the Fairy Godmother said, and she handed the little girl a box. Inside was a brand-new magic wand. "Now we can begin your advanced fairy training."

"Hooray!" shouted Eliza.

"Could the first lesson be how to clean up a messy garden?" Cinderella asked with a smile.

Eliza gave Cinderella a big hug. "The next time I visit, I promise I'll be able to undo my spells," she said.

Then the Fairy Godmother began to straighten up the garden—with the help of some magic, of course.